The Enormous Turnip

retold and illustrated
by Kathy Parkinson

ALBERT WHITMAN & COMPANY, MORTON GROVE, ILLINOIS

Library of Congress Cataloging-in-Publication Data

Parkinson, Kathy.
The enormous turnip.
Summary: One of Grandfather's turnips grows to
such an enormous size that the whole family including
the dog, cat, and mouse try in vain to pull it up.
[1. Folklore—Soviet Union.]   I. Title.
PZ8.1.P225En   1986   398.2'1'0947   [E]   85-14432
ISBN 0-8075-2062-4 (lib. bdg.)

The text of this book is printed in sixteen-point Caslon.

For John

Grandfather Ivan planted a turnip in the garden.

It grew and it grew and it GREW.
When the time came to pull it up,

the turnip was ENORMOUS!

Grandfather took hold of the stem.
He pulled and he pulled and he pulled,

but the turnip would not budge.
It was stuck fast.

"Grandmother!" he called.
"Come and help me pull our turnip!"
Grandmother Luba ran to help.
She wrapped her arms around Grandfather's waist.
Grandmother pulled Grandfather while he tugged on the turnip.

They pulled and they pulled and they pulled,

but the enormous turnip did not budge.
It was stuck fast.

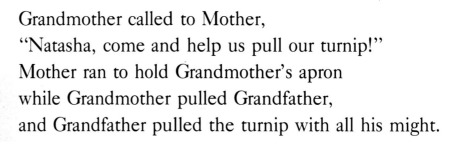

Grandmother called to Mother,
"Natasha, come and help us pull our turnip!"
Mother ran to hold Grandmother's apron
while Grandmother pulled Grandfather,
and Grandfather pulled the turnip with all his might.

They pulled and they pulled and they pulled,

but still the turnip did not move.
"Olga! Olga!" called Mother to her daughter,
"Come and help us pull our turnip!"

Little Olga ran as fast as she could.
She held on to Mother,
while Mother pulled Grandmother,
Grandmother pulled Grandfather,
and Grandfather tugged the turnip
with all his might.

They pulled and they pulled and they pulled,

but still they could not move it.
The enormous turnip was stuck fast.
"Alyosha! Alyosha!" called Olga to her puppy,
"Come and help us pull our turnip!"

Alyosha barked loudly.
He ran and took Olga's dress in his teeth.
He pulled little Olga,
while Olga pulled Mother,
Mother pulled Grandmother,
Grandmother pulled Grandfather,
and Grandfather pulled the turnip
with all his might.

but even now the turnip would not move.
It was stuck fast.

the mouse heard all the noise.
k! Squeak!" she cried and ran from her hole.
sped the fur of Anya the kitten.
 pulled Anya,
ulled Alyosha,
 pulled little Olga,
lled Mother,
 pulled Grandmother,
y all pulled Grandfather,
ffed and puffed as he tugged
 his might.

They pulled and they pulled and they pulled,

but still the turnip would not budge.
It was stuck fast.

Alyosha called to Anya the kitten,
"Come and help us pull our turnip!"
"Meow! Meow!" mewed Anya.
She took Alyosha's tail in her paws.
Anya pulled Alyosha,
Alyosha pulled little Olga,
Olga pulled Mother,
Mother pulled Grandmother,
Grandmother pulled Grandfather,
while Grandfather tugged and tugged with all his might.

Many
"Sque
She g
Many
Anya
Alyos
Olga
Moth
and t
who l
with

They pulled and they pulled and they pulled,

They pulled and they pulled and they pulled,

but the turnip would not budge.
It was stuck just as fast as before.

Now Petya the beetle crawled off a leaf.
He took the tail of Manya the mouse.
Petya pulled Manya,
Manya pulled Anya,
Anya pulled Alyosha,
Alyosha pulled little Olga,
Olga pulled Mother,
Mother pulled Grandmother,
and they all pulled Grandfather,
who tugged and tugged on the enormous turnip.

They pulled,

and they pulled,

and they PULLED!

WHOA-OOMP!
They pulled that enormous turnip right out of the ground!

The turnip landed on Grandfather!
He fell on Grandmother,
Grandmother fell on Mother,
Mother fell on little Olga,
Olga fell on Alyosha the puppy,
Alyosha fell on Anya the kitten,
Anya fell on Manya the mouse,
but luckily Petya the beetle ran away
before anyone fell on him!

That night they all had an *enormous* turnip dinner,

and everyone went right to bed,
including Petya the beetle.

"How strong I am!" he thought,
and he fell fast asleep.